THOMAS CRANE PUBLIC LIBRARY

QUINCY MASS

CITY APPROPRIATION

ANIMAL ANTICS A TO Z®

Yoko Yak's Yakety Yakking

by Barbara deRubertis • illustrated by R.W. Alley

THE KANE PRESS / NEW YORK

Alpha Betty's Class

Nina Nandu
Oliver Otter
Polly Porcupine
Quentin Quokka
Rosie Raccoon
Sammy Skunk
Tessa Tiger
Umma Ungka
Victor Vicuna
Walter Warthog
Xavier Ox
Yoko Yak
STAR of the BOOK
Zachary Zebra
Alpha Betty

Library of Congress Cataloging-in-Publication Data

deRubertis, Barbara.
Yoko Yak's yakety yakking / by Barbara deRubertis ; illustrated by R.W. Alley.
p. cm. — (Animal antics A to Z)
Summary: Yoko Yak is eager to talk about her first kayak trip, but Alpha Betty tells her she must wait, challenging the chatty student to find another way to tell her classmates about the experience.
ISBN 978-1-57565-358-7 (library binding : alk. paper) — ISBN 978-1-57565-350-1 (pbk. : alk. paper) — ISBN 978-1-57565-389-1 (e-book)
[1. Quietude—Fiction. 2. Schools—Fiction. 3. Yak—Fiction. 4. Animals—Fiction. 5. Alphabet.]
I. Alley, R. W. (Robert W.), ill. II. Title.
PZ7.D4475Yok 2011
[E]—dc22 2010051473

1 3 5 7 9 10 8 6 4 2

First published in the United States of America in 2011 by Kane Press, Inc.
Printed in the United States of America
WOZ0711

Series Editor: Juliana Hanford
Book Design: Edward Miller

www.kanepress.com

Yoko Yak yanked back the covers and bounced out of bed.

She had SO much to tell her friends about her adventure yesterday!

“Yodel-odel-odel!” Yoko sang in the shower.

“Yay for school today!” Yoko chanted as she dressed.

Mama Yak called to Yoko.
"Are you ready for breakfast?"

"Yip! Yap! Yup!" Yoko yelled back.

“Yogurt’s yum, yum, yummy in my tum, tum, tummy,” Yoko chattered as she ate.

“Don’t talk with your mouth full, Yoko,” said Papa Yak.

"Don't talk, period. Please!" said Yoko's younger sister, Yolanda. "You're always yakety yakking."

"I am ***not***!" Yoko yelped.

Yoko zipped into the yard at
Alpha Betty's school.

"Yo, Polly!" she yelled.
"Yo, Sammy! Yo, Bobby!
I went KAYAKING yesterday!"

Alpha Betty rang the bell. She smiled at Yoko.

"We all want to hear about your kayak adventure!
Today is a very busy day.
But tomorrow afternoon we'll have sharing time.
You can tell us about your trip then!"

But Yoko couldn't wait. She started telling Polly Porcupine about the kayak trip during math.
"We kayaked down Coyote Canyon!" said Yoko.

"Shh!" whispered Polly.
"We're supposed to be doing math!"

During silent reading time, Yoko started telling Sammy Skunk about the kayak trip.

Sammy put his finger up to his lips. “We’re supposed to be reading ***silently***!”

Next it was time for art.
Alpha Betty smiled at Yoko.
"You can draw a picture of your kayak trip!"

"Okay!" said Yoko.

But Yoko also wanted to ***talk*** about her kayak trip.
She started whispering to Bobby Baboon.

Bobby put a hand over his ear.
"I can't think when you're yakking in my ear, Yoko.
You're a very yakety yak today!"

Yoko burst into tears.
Alpha Betty hurried back to Yoko's desk.
"Bobby called me a ***yakety*** yak!" Yoko yowled.

Bobby said, "I'm sorry, Yoko! I DO want to
hear about your kayak trip. But not right now!"

Alpha Betty whispered to Yoko, "Tell us about
your trip with your drawing! And IF you can
be a quiet little yak during class time . . .
you may talk ***first*** during sharing time tomorrow!"

The next morning, Yoko was early for breakfast.
She was wearing her Coyote Canyon T-shirt.
She was holding her Coyote Canyon yo-yo.
And . . . she was absolutely ***quiet***!

Yolanda looked at Yoko. Then she looked at Papa.
"What's wrong with Yoko? She's not yakking!"

Yoko dipped her toast in egg yolk
and popped it in her mouth.

She smiled at Yolanda as she chewed . . .
with her mouth shut.

When Yoko arrived at school, she smiled and waved at her friends.

She smiled and waved at Alpha Betty.

Yoko waited for math to begin.
She was very quiet.

"Are you okay?" asked Polly Porcupine.

Yoko nodded *yes* . . . and said nothing.

During reading, Yoko was ***also*** very quiet.

"Are you okay?" asked Sammy Skunk.

Yoko nodded *yes* . . . and said nothing.

When it was time for art, Yoko was ***still*** very quiet.

"Are you okay?" asked Bobby Baboon.

Yoko nodded *yes* . . . and said nothing.

Finally, it was sharing time.
Alpha Betty announced, "Yoko, you may go first!"

Yoko ran to the front of the classroom.
She smiled. And she said . . . NOTHING!

She showed everyone her two drawings of kayaks.

She pointed to her yellow Coyote Canyon T-shirt.

She demonstrated her yellow Coyote Canyon yo-yo.

All without saying a ***word***!

The class began laughing and chanting.
"Yakety Yak, please come back!
Yakety Yak, please come back!"

Yoko Yak laughed, too.

And then . . . she began to TALK!

"My kayak BOUNCED over waves!
I was SOAKED by water spray! And when
I yelled, it ECHOED in Coyote Canyon!

But I CAN be a ***quiet*** yak . . . as well as a ***yakety*** yak.
And I made up a yodel about it last night!"

"Yodel for us, Yoko!" yelled the class.

First Yoko whispered:

Then Yoko chanted loudly:

“Yay for you, Yoko Yak!” cried Alpha Betty.
“You proved you CAN be a quiet yak!”

“And a clever yak!” said Polly.
“And a funny yak!” said Sammy.
“And a yodeling yak!” laughed Bobby.

Then everyone cheered, "Yay for Yoko Yak!"

And *everyone* did the "Yakety Yak Yodel"!

FUN FACTS

- Home: Wild yaks live in the Tibet region of China and nearby. They prefer high areas where the weather is cold.
- Family: Female yaks and young yaks live together in large herds. Adult male yaks live in small groups or alone. If a herd is disturbed, the yaks will gallop away with their tails held straight up in the air!
- Size: Wild yaks can grow to a height of 6 feet at the top of their shoulder hump. Their horns can each be 3 feet long.
- Appearance: Most of a yak's hair is short. But the hair on its sides can be so long and shaggy it almost reaches the ground!
- **Did You Know?** Yaks often crunch on ice and snow to get water. And they can use their horns to break through the ice and snow when they are looking for grass to eat!

LOOK BACK

Learning to identify letter sounds (phonemes) at the beginning, middle, and end of words is called "phonemic awareness."

- The word ***yak*** begins with the *y consonant** sound. Listen to the words on page 9 being read again. When you hear a word that begins with the *y* sound, repeat the word while you stand up and make a giant **Y** by raising your arms in the air! Then quickly sit down again.
- The word ***kayak*** has the *y consonant* sound in the middle. Listen to the words on page 25 being read again. When you hear a word that has the *y* sound in the middle, repeat the word and pretend to paddle a kayak.

*Note: *Y* can have a consonant sound *or* a vowel sound (like the long ***i*** or the long ***e*** sound). In the activities for this book, we will practice finding only the consonant sound for *y*.

TRY THIS!

Yak with Yoko Yak!

Listen carefully as each word in the word bank is read aloud.

- If the word begins with the *y* sound, stand up, say "YAKETY YAK!," and sit down again.
- If the word does NOT begin with the *y* sound, remain seated and say *nothing*!

yak yarn fun yogurt draw
read yam you math year bell
yawn talk trip yolk yard quiet
young yes yodel

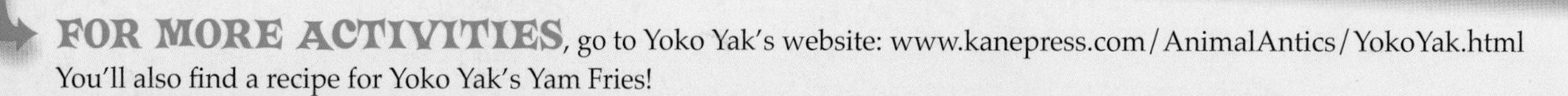

FOR MORE ACTIVITIES, go to Yoko Yak's website: www.kanepress.com/AnimalAntics/YokoYak.html
You'll also find a recipe for Yoko Yak's Yam Fries!